The House With No Name

by P. Goodhart

illustrated by Brett Hawkins

Librarian Reviewer
Kathleen Baxter
Children's Literature Consultant
formerly with Anoka County Library, MN
BA College of Saint Catherine, St. Paul, MN
MA in Library Science, University of Minnesota

Reading Consultant
Elizabeth Stedem
Educator/Consultant, Colorado Springs, CO
MA in Elementary Education, University of Denver, CO

 STONE ARCH BOOKS
Minneapolis   San Diego

First published in the United States in 2007
by Stone Arch Books,
151 Good Counsel Drive, P.O. Box 669,
Mankato, Minnesota 56002.
www.stonearchbooks.com

Published by arrangement with
Barrington Stoke Ltd, Edinburgh.

Library of Congress Cataloging-in-Publication Data
Goodhart, Pippa.
　　The House with No Name / by P. Goodhart; illustrated by Brett
Hawkins.
　　　p. cm. — (Pathway Books)
　　　Summary: When his family moves to a remote house in the woods that
has stood empty for years, Jamie feels there is something very strange about
the place, but soon makes friends with Colin who has lived nearby for years
and years.
　　　ISBN-13: 978-1-59889-103-4 (hardcover)
　　　ISBN-10: 1-59889-103-0 (hardcover)
　　　ISBN-13: 978-1-59889-270-3 (paperback)
　　　ISBN-10: 1-59889-270-3 (paperback)
　　　[1. Ghosts—Fiction. 2. Dwellings—Fiction. 3. Moving, Household—
Fiction.] I. Hawkins, Brett, ill. II. Title. III. Series.
　PZ7.G6125Hou 2007
　[Fic]—dc22　　　　　　　　　　　　　　　　　　　　　2006007175

Art Director: Heather Kindseth
Graphic Designer: Kay Fraser

1　2　3　4　5　6　11　10　09　08　07　06

Printed in the United States of America.

TABLE OF CONTENTS

Chapter 1
THE HOUSE

"What's the house like? Is it cool?" Jamie asked.

"You'll see soon," said Jamie's dad.

"Can I have my own room?"

"A small one, yes," said Dad. "The girls will share the biggest bedroom, and Mom and I will have the other."

Jamie sat smiling in the front seat. When Mom was around, he had to sit with his sisters in the back seat.

Today it was just him and his dad.

Jamie held the map on his lap.
The back of the van was full of tools,
sleeping bags, and food.

"So what is the house like? Mom
says it's falling down!" said Jamie.

"We hired a local builder to look at
it, and he says it's in good shape. We
just have to paint the place and put in
new wiring. Then it'll feel like home!
Now, watch for a side road on the left,"
Dad said.

Soon, they turned off the main road
and drove down a long tunnel of trees.

"This house is miles from anywhere!"
said Jamie.

"You have a bike," his father said.

"It'll be dark at night," said Jamie.

Jamie was used to the streetlights in town. The thought of biking down this road after dark made him shiver. Then the van bumped out of the tunnel of trees into the sunlight.

"There's our new home!" said Dad. "What do you think of it?"

It was the kind of house Jamie's sisters drew — a square with a door in the middle, a window at each corner, and a high roof.

"It looks like a face!" said Jamie.

"Don't be silly!" said Dad as he took the bag of tools from the van.

"Go take a quick look around. Then come back and help me carry these tools inside," said his dad.

The house did look like a face. The
roof was like hair. The two upstairs
windows were like winking eyes. The
windows downstairs had dark red
boards over them. They looked like
rosy cheeks. The red door was the
mouth and the porch roof over it was
the nose.

Jamie ran from empty room to
empty room. The house felt alive. He
frowned and went to find his dad.

They went into the kitchen. It looked
clean and tidy. Jamie's dad looked
around, puzzled.

"You'd never think that there was
an explosion in this room, would
you?" he said.

"An explosion?" Jamie asked.

"Yes. Years ago. Someone was killed."

Dad hung Jamie's cap from a nail on the back of the door.

"There," said Dad. "As my mom always said, when you've hung up your cap, you're at home. Would you like to have a campfire tonight?"

"Yeah, great!" said Jamie, smiling and putting his cap back on.

"But now we've got to fix this window." Dad took out his hammer.

"When was the explosion?" asked Jamie.

"About thirty-five years ago," said his dad. "A gas heater blew up. The family moved out after that, and the house has been empty ever since."

"Why didn't anyone else want the place?" asked Jamie.

"Well," said Dad, "it's miles from anywhere. Houses like to have other houses around them."

Jamie grinned. "Now you're talking as if houses were people. Mom's the same. She said this place needed cheering up."

Dad smiled. "She's right. The house seems sad."

"Yeah. Almost like it's frozen in time," said Jamie. "I think the house wants to be lived in again. I like it."

"Good," said Dad. "Now, go and get me a board to hold the door open, will you?"

As Jamie was looking inside the van for a board, a cold shiver went down his spine. He felt he was being watched.

He spun around to look. There was nothing there.

That's odd, he thought, and hurried back into the house with the board.

Jamie went back into the house and kept Dad talking. That way he could forget the scary feeling that someone was watching him. "I've always wanted to live in the woods," said Dad.

"Why?" asked Jamie.

"When I was little, we always lived in towns," said Dad. "We moved a lot. I wanted to settle in the country. I had to wait a long time. But when Grandma died last year and left us some money, I found this place. And here we are."

"I think my parents were always moving from house to house to escape their sadness. You see, I had a brother who died. Your grandma and granddad loved him so much," Dad added.

"More than they loved you?" asked Jamie.

"They didn't want me to think that," said Dad. "They didn't like to talk about him, but I always felt that he had been closer to them."

"Dad," began Jamie, "I'll have to make new friends now, won't I? And we don't have an address or a phone number yet!"

"We'll soon take care of that. What should we call the house? Woodside? Or Rose Cottage?"

"Boring," said Jamie. "It needs a better name than that."

"What, then?" asked Dad.

"I'll think about it," said Jamie.

Jamie and his dad worked through the morning, mending the kitchen windows.

Again, Jamie felt like he was being watched, but he didn't see anyone.

"Did you hear something just now?" he asked his dad.

"No," Dad said.

Jamie was sure that someone outside was looking in at him. "I'll tell you a joke, Dad," he said at last. "What has the bottom at its top?"

"Mmm, I give up," his dad said.

Then a voice from outside said, "Easy! A leg has a bottom at its top!"

A boy was looking in at the window and he was laughing.

Chapter 2
COLIN

"Hello," said the boy. "Are you like the others who came to look around or are you really going to live here?"

"Hi," said Dad. "Jamie and I are doing some work on the house before the rest of the family gets here. He was just asking if there might be any other boys living around here. Do you live nearby?"

"Yes," said the boy.

The boy wore a t-shirt, jeans, and brown shoes. He had red cheeks and messy blond hair. He made Jamie think of someone, but he wasn't sure who it was.

Jamie wanted to ask the boy if he'd been watching them all morning. Instead, all he said was, "Do you know any other jokes?"

The boy grinned. "What's black and white and black and white and black and white?"

"I don't know," said Jamie.

"A penguin rolling down a hill!" said the boy.

"What's this?" said Jamie. He wagged his little finger.

"A worm?" asked the boy.

"No! A microwave!" said Jamie.

"A what?" asked the boy with a puzzled look.

"Don't you get it? A microwave. You know, a very small wave!"

"Oh." The boy looked blank.

"Don't you have microwave ovens around here?" asked Jamie.

It was clear that the boy didn't know what Jamie was talking about. Perhaps they lived in the past around here, thought Jamie.

His dad winked at him. Then Dad smiled at them both.

"I'll leave you two jokers alone, and I'll get us all some lunch. I saw a burger place in town," said Dad.

"Would you like to have lunch with us?" he asked the boy.

The boy smiled. "Yes, please. I haven't had hamburgers for years and years and years!"

"What's your name?" asked Jamie.

"Colin."

"How old are you?"

"Eleven. I should have been twelve pretty soon," said Colin.

"Should have been?" said Jamie. "Going to be, you mean. Same as me! I'll be twelve next week. Have you lived around here long?"

"Yes, years and years," said Colin.

"Who were the others you said came to look at the house?" Jamie asked.

"They wanted to knock down this house and build a new one." Colin seemed angry.

"So why didn't they?" asked Jamie.

"They gave up and went away," Colin said.

"Oh," Jamie said.

He thought Colin was a little strange, but he was the right age, so maybe they could be friends. At least Jamie and Colin could hang out.

"Which school do you go to?" Jamie asked. "I'm going to the local public school this year."

"I go to the private school," said Colin. "I had to pass tests to get in. I wanted to be an astronaut."

"Don't you think it would be great to land on the moon? They're planning to do that, you know!" said Colin.

"Don't be silly!" said Jamie. "They did that years ago! Now they want to send someone to Mars."

"You'd see the world from far away, and you'd be free!" Colin went on.

"I think you're nuts!" said Jamie. "It would be too lonely out in space."

"It'd be beautiful," said Colin. "You'd see the world like a tiny ball in the sky."

"Wouldn't that scare you?" asked Jamie.

"It'd be worth it, to escape," said Colin sadly.

"Escape from what?" Jamie asked. He thought of his grandma and granddad and their sad life of always moving on. "You can't escape from your feelings by going far away. Feelings always go with you."

Chapter 3
TROUBLE

"Burgers coming up," called Jamie's dad as he stepped out of the van.

Jamie was glad to see food and to have Dad back.

"Sit down on that log and we'll eat," his dad said.

Dad looked over at Colin. "Do you need to call your mom and tell her where you are?"

Colin shook his head. "No one will miss me." He held up a burger and then bit into it slowly. His eyes closed. "Mmmm!"

Jamie laughed, "It's only a burger, you know!" Then he said to his dad, "Guess what? Colin wants to be an astronaut!"

"Or a bird," said Colin. "I just want to be free to go up and away."

Colin knew all about birds and animals and plants.

"Why don't you take Jamie into the woods and show him around?" said Dad. "I'll finish the windows. My friend is coming tomorrow to help me with the electrical wiring. There's not much more we can do before then."

"You two go and explore," said Dad. "Bring back some dry sticks for a camp fire. Are you going to join us for supper, Colin?"

"I'd like that," said Colin.

Colin led Jamie into the woods. "I'll show you where to find pine cones to get the fire started."

* * *

The woods all looked the same to Jamie, lots of trees and branches, and paths leading everywhere.

"It sure would be easy to get lost in here," he said.

Colin showed him how to figure out where he was by checking the sun's location in the sky. Then he showed Jamie lots of plants and birds.

He pointed out the different tracks that the animals made.

"And look at these!" said Colin. "Do you know what these are?"

"Yes, I do know. Ferns!" said Jamie. But Colin was pointing to something on one of the leaves.

"See that? Butterfly eggs. Just hatching," said Colin.

"No kidding! The caterpillars are so tiny!" said Jamie.

"Sometimes I feel like a caterpillar," said Colin. "I'd rather be a butterfly. I would have to make a big cocoon for myself first."

"You say some weird things," said Jamie.

"Have you ever watched a butterfly hatch from a cocoon?" asked Colin.

Jamie shook his head.

"I have," said Colin. "They come out all folded up. They look like they'll never be able to fly. But the sun warms them and that makes them stretch their wings out wide. Then they flap their wings and they're off." Colin gave a sigh.

"So you really do want to fly?" asked Jamie.

"More than anything. I want to go up and away and be free," said Colin. "See that?"

He pointed to some tall, pink flowers.

"I call it the rocket plant. They look like rockets ready to take off. Aren't they great?" Colin said.

Jamie looked at Colin to see if he was joking. None of his old friends would have talked about flowers.

But Colin wasn't joking. And he was right. The flowers were great.

"What's that?" asked Jamie as something made a noise in the trees.

"It's a woodpecker," said Colin. "Don't you know any bird noises? You do have birds in the city, don't you?"

"Yes," replied Jamie. "Pigeons and sparrows. I know what cuckoos sound like. I heard them when we visited Europe last summer."

"I hate cuckoos," said Colin. "They lay their eggs in other birds' nests. The poor mother bird has to go on feeding the great big cuckoo chick, even when it gets bigger than she is. And it pushes her own chicks out of the nest."

Colin stopped to pick up a stick. Then he said, "I called my little brother Cuckoo. He was adopted."

"I only have sisters," said Jamie.

"Cuckoo was a baby when he came to us. Mom and Dad thought he was great. He took up all of Mom's and Dad's time, so there was none left over for me," said Colin.

"Didn't you like him at all?" asked Jamie.

"Oh, yeah! As he grew bigger I showed him things, how to swim and climb trees, that kind of thing. I loved him, and I hated him at the same time, you know?" said Colin.

Jamie laughed. "I know."

Then Colin looked at Jamie. "Have you ever really hated somebody, even just for a second? Did you tell them you hated them? Did you even say that you wished they were dead?"

Jamie nodded. "Yes. You can hate someone for doing something, but still love them. It gets mixed up."

"That's it! It was like that with me," shouted Colin.

"What do you mean?" asked Jamie.

Colin pointed to an old log.

"See those marks?" asked Colin.

Jamie could see marks cut into the side of the log.

"There's a C and a T," Colin told him. "C for me and a T for my brother. I let my brother use my knife to make his T. He was too little and he cut himself. I think I killed him."

"You what?" Jamie felt cold.

"I think I killed my brother," said Colin.

"Did you kill your brother or not?" asked Jamie.

"I don't know!" shouted Colin.

"Then go home and find out!" said Jamie. "I bet he's fine! Is that why you ran away?"

Colin felt the C and the T in the wood with his finger.

Jamie saw that the marks were old.

"Look, if you are in trouble, you can stay with us tonight," said Jamie. "Dad will help you figure it out. He's got his cell phone with him."

Colin looked puzzled but said nothing. They found some sticks for the campfire. Colin gave a sudden yell and put his hands to his head.

"What's up?" asked Jamie.

Colin looked at his hands in horror. His fingers held a small tuft of hair.

"How did that happen?" said Jamie.

With a wild cry, Colin ran toward the house. What was the matter? Jamie wondered. Was he feeling sick?

There was a sudden shout and a terrible crash. Jamie ran after Colin. "Dad!" cried Jamie.

Chapter 4
DAD

An empty ladder was leaning against the house.

Colin stood below it, his hands pressed to his mouth as if he was trying not to scream.

On the ground lay Jamie's dad.

"Dad! What happened? Are you hurt?" Jamie was scared. He put a hand on his dad's arm.

Dad opened his eyes. He was shaking. "My leg," he said. Then he closed his eyes again in pain.

"Don't move!" Jamie told him. "You might have hurt your back."

Dad's right leg was bent at a funny angle. "Colin, call an ambulance. Quick!" Jamie said.

Colin looked confused. Jamie grabbed his dad's cell phone and dialed 911.

"What happened?" Jamie asked his dad after he hung up the phone.

"I was on the ladder, just pulling out a broken shingle from the roof. Then something made me fall."

"Was it Colin? Did he do it?" asked Jamie.

"No! Colin came running from the woods just as I fell. He was shocked, poor kid," said his dad.

"You could have died," said Jamie.

"I know, Jamie. But I didn't, and I'm not going to," said Dad. "It's just my leg. You'll have to get in touch with your mom and go back home."

Jamie held his dad's hand. He told him they'd make the house into the best home ever. Then, Jamie heard the ambulance siren.

The paramedics lifted Dad onto a stretcher and put him into the ambulance.

"Will he be all right?" asked Jamie.

"He'll be fine, but what about you?" asked a paramedic.

"I'm going to call my mom and go back home," said Jamie.

"Good plan," replied the paramedic.

As they drove away, Jamie felt awful. "I have to call my mom."

"Why not stay here?" asked Colin.

"Here? All by myself?" said Jamie. He was shocked.

"I'll be here," Colin told him.

"Do you think my mom would let me?" asked Jamie.

Jamie called home, told his mom about the accident, and asked if he could stay with a friend. He didn't tell his mom that he would be alone in the house with Colin.

"Has Dad met Colin?" she asked.

"Yes. He likes Colin," Jamie told her.

"All right then. I'll pick you up tomorrow. Where does Colin live?"

"Don't worry about that, Mom. I'll be at our new house when you come over," said Jamie.

"Okay, Jamie. Bye," Mom said.

Chapter 5
CAMP FIRE

"Did you run away from home?" Jamie asked Colin. "I've thought about doing that."

"I'm not where I should be," Colin told him.

Jamie smiled, "So I'm going to spend a night with a ghost and a runaway!"

"Why do you say there's a ghost?" asked Colin.

"Somebody told my mom there was a ghost in the house," said Jamie.

"You don't seem to mind," said Colin.

"I don't." Now that Colin was with him, the place didn't seem so spooky.

"Let's light the fire," said Colin.

"Good idea," said Jamie. "The matches are in the van. There's some hot dogs and drinks, too. Dad even remembered to bring a can opener for the beans."

Colin knew about making camp fires. "I was in Boy Scouts," he told Jamie as the flames shot up from the sticks.

"Hungry?" asked Jamie.

"Starving!" said Colin.

"I haven't had a grilled hot dog for years and years!" said Jamie.

Colin looked up at the house. "You told me your dad wasn't going to hurt the house, but he was pulling it apart!"

"He only pulled out a broken piece of shingle. What's wrong with that?" asked Jamie.

Colin stared up at the roof and put a hand to his head.

He's getting weird again, thought Jamie. "You get the bread out and I'll open the beans," he told Colin.

As they ate, it began to get dark.

The fire died down.

"I'll take the flashlight and get the sleeping bags from the van," said Jamie.

Chapter 6
GHOSTS?

The boys put the sleeping bags on the floor of the front bedroom.

Jamie could hear noises all around. The house creaked and its pipes hummed. The wind howled down the chimney. A sudden yipping sound made Jamie gasp.

"That's only a fox," said Colin. "Sometimes they sound like small boys yelling," he explained.

"It's all right," said Jamie. "I didn't think it was a ghost. I don't think this house is spooky," he lied.

Colin said nothing, so Jamie asked, "Do you think there are ghosts?"

"Yes," said Colin.

"Are you sure?" Jamie switched on his flashlight so that he could see Colin's face.

"You might not believe in ghosts," said Colin, "but the ghosts believe in you."

"Oh, ha ha! Are you trying to scare me?" Jamie said, laughing.

Colin whispered, "No."

Jamie sat up in his sleeping bag and waved the flashlight. "I can zap all the ghosts with this," he said.

Jamie shined the light into Colin's face again. Colin's skin was so pale you could almost see through it. "You look like you've seen a ghost!" said Jamie.

"I have. Lots of times," Colin said.

"What, here?" asked Jamie.

"Yes," Colin told him.

Jamie almost choked. "What's it like then, this ghost? How old is it?"

"About our age," said Colin.

"No! I mean, when did it live? Does it walk around in armor? Does it walk through walls?" asked Jamie.

"No," Colin said.

"Then what? What does its face look like?" Jamie wanted to know.

Colin said, "I can't tell you. I haven't seen its face."

"A ghost without a head?" Jamie laughed.

"No." Colin looked at Jamie. "I'll tell you about it."

Colin began. "There was once a man and woman who loved each other. They lived in this house in the woods, and they wanted children."

"Is this a fairy tale?" asked Jamie.

"Do you want to hear it, or not?"

"Yeah. Go on," Jamie said.

"Well, they had a baby boy," said Colin. "He grew up and went to school and learned to swim and went fishing. The man and woman waited nine years for another baby, but none came. So they asked the boy if he would like them to adopt a baby."

Colin took a deep breath.

"The boy knew how much his mom and dad wanted another baby, so he said yes. The baby came, and it was a boy. The baby took the older boy's toys," Colin went on. "He cried all night. Mom and Dad were always busy looking after him."

"There was no time for any more fishing trips," he said sadly. "Mom was always feeding the baby or cleaning him or playing with him. Dad worked hard to pay for the extra things they needed. The bigger boy felt left out."

"Was the baby called Cuckoo?" asked Jamie.

"Yes." Colin's face was paper pale. "The one I killed."

"He cut himself with your knife by mistake?" asked Jamie.

"No. It wasn't then. I killed him later, and it wasn't a mistake. I meant to hurt him, but not to kill him." Colin's eyes were wide with pain.

Jamie put a hand on Colin's knee. "How did it happen?" Jamie asked.

"Cuckoo was four years old," said Colin. "One day he went into my room, and he took the model rocket I made. He took it, and he got Mom's rolling pin, and he hit it and hit it. It was smashed to pieces. When I found what he did, I wanted to smash him."

"I would have felt the same way," said Jamie, but Colin didn't hear him.

"Cuckoo was out on the swing under the ash tree. He saw me." Jamie wished Colin would stop.

Colin went on, "He shouted for me to look how high he could go. He didn't understand how angry I was about the smashed rocket. I wanted so badly to hurt him, to make him cry like I was crying."

"You're crying now," said Jamie.

"It was easy to kill him," Colin said. "I just shouted his name and waved."

"Waved?" asked Jamie.

"Yes. With both hands. You see, we had a game where if I did something, held my nose or hopped on one leg or something, he'd copy me. This time I waved with both hands, and he copied me. Then he fell off the swing."

"Then what happened?" asked Jamie.

"I saw him fall. I was happy. Then he landed on the ground and shouted. The next moment my hate exploded, and we were all dead."

"Hate doesn't explode!" Jamie froze. "When was this, Colin?"

"Cuckoo died in 1965," said Colin.

"Dad told me that a gas heater exploded here in 1965. One person died," said Jamie.

Colin put his hands over his ears. "No! Don't tell me! I can't stand it!" He was shaking. "Everything stopped when my hate exploded! I don't want to know what happened next! I have kept things the same here for years and years and years."

"You scared away anyone who came here?" asked Jamie.

"Yes!" said Colin.

"Did you make my dad fall off the ladder?" asked Jamie.

"I don't know. Maybe! I didn't want to, but I make bad things happen," said Colin.

"Your dad was pulling out my hair when he pulled the shingle. It hurt me. I shouted for him to stop, but that was all!" said Colin.

Colin's eyes were sad. "I think I can kill people without coming near them, Jamie. I did that to Cuckoo and to my mom and dad. And now your dad."

"My dad's not dead, Colin," said Jamie. Then something clicked in Jamie's mind. "Did you say that Dad was pulling out your hair?"

"Yes. Pulling out great hunks of it."

"Colin, is this house you?" Jamie asked very softly.

Colin nodded. "Yes. The house is me. And I'm the ghost."

Chapter 7
EXPLODING FREE

What Colin said still didn't make sense to Jamie.

"Dad said that only one person died when the gas exploded," Jamie said. "And it had nothing to do with anyone hating anyone else."

"I was there," said Colin. "I know. My hate exploded and killed Terry and my parents."

"Who?" Jamie sat up.

"What name did you say, Colin?"

"Terry," said Colin.

"Is that Cuckoo's real name?" asked Jamie.

"Yes," said Colin.

Jamie felt cold. "My dad's name is Terry!" shouted Jamie.

Colin looked confused. "So what?"

Jamie got out of his sleeping bag and went over to Colin. He crouched down beside him. "My dad was adopted," he said. "Did your brother Terry have dark hair like my dad? Is your family's last name Hall?"

Colin sat up. Jamie could see in his eyes that the answer was yes. "My dad must be your brother!" shouted Jamie.

Jamie clapped his hands. "He must be! And he's alive, and his mom and dad were alive until not long ago. My grandma — your mom — only died last year. *You* were the only one killed in that explosion!"

Jamie jumped up from his sleeping bag and went over to the window. It was just getting light. Out in the yard, a small boy swung back and forth under the big ash tree. Sunlight shined through the window. It shined right through Colin as if he wasn't there and lit up the floor under him.

Colin had no shadow.

Jamie went over to him. He put out a hand to touch Colin, but there was nothing there.

"Don't go," said Jamie. "Look out the window. It's Cuckoo on the swing!"

The small boy was leaning back and forth to make himself swing higher.

"Just watch," Jamie told Colin. "You'll see. He'll be okay."

It was like watching a silent movie.

The boy on the swing looked up at the house and shouted. His mouth was open, but there was no sound. He let go of the ropes on the swing and waved with both hands. Then he fell.

"Quick!" Jamie ran down the stairs, opened the door, and raced over to the small child. Colin's mom and dad were there already. The little boy sat up. He was crying. His parents held out their arms to the child.

At that same moment, there was a terrible booming sound and Jamie was thrown to the ground. For a moment Jamie lay in the grass, stunned and unable to think. But as he came to, he knew what that booming sound was.

"Colin!" he shouted. "Colin, your mom and dad didn't die. You saved them! When Terry fell, they ran outside, so they weren't in the house when the gas exploded. You didn't kill anybody, Colin. You saved them all, and they loved you always!"

Jamie looked up. He was alone. Then Jamie saw that the house had exploded. Colin was free. It was exciting, beautiful, and terrible.

Chapter 8
PEACE

Jamie sat, stunned. The house was just a pile of rubble. It lay there at peace. The only sound now was the song of the birds.

"Are you free now, Colin?" Jamie asked the air.

The house felt peaceful, the house that was Colin. All the sadness was gone, and the sun was shining.

Jamie slowly got up.

Then he ran into the woods and found the place where the pink rocket flowers grew.

He picked them until his hands were sore.

He took the flowers back to the house that had been Colin.

He found the place where the fireplace used to be.

Part of the chimney still stood among the rubble.

Jamie stuck the rocket flowers into the broken chimney as if it were a vase.

Then he stood looking up at the sky and thought of birds and butterflies and people. He thought of space rockets.

"Goodbye, Colin," he said. "I'll tell Dad, I mean, tell Cuckoo, about you. We'll make a new house and live here always," said Jamie.

Jamie knew that he would find Colin in the birds and flowers and stars around their new home.

Colin would be a part of this place forever.

About the Author

Pippa Goodhart grew up in a small town that had only two classes in the whole school. She was a slow reader as a student, but always enjoyed creating stories with her friends. She studied to be a teacher, and then worked in a children's bookstore. Goodhart now lives in Leicester, England with her husband.

About the Illustrator

Brett Hawkins was born in Albert Lea, Minnesota and currently lives just west of Minneapolis. He can't remember a time that he wasn't drawing or painting or sculpting. "I've always had a vivid imagination," he says, "and illustrating is probably my favorite way to bring those images in my mind to life." Hawkins finds inspiration everywhere he turns: family, friends, music, and other artist's work. His favorite artist? He has too many, but he especially likes American illustrators, such as N. C. Wyeth.

Glossary

assured (a-SHERD)—promised or guaranteed

clank (KLANGK)—a sharp, hard metallic sound

cuckoo (KOO-koo)—a bird that lays eggs in other birds' nests

paramedic (pare-uh-MED-ik)—a person who gives medical treatment, but is not a nurse or a doctor

rubble (RUHB-uhl)—broken bricks, stones or pieces of wood. A pile of rubble was all that remained of the house after the explosion.

shingle (SHING-guhl)—a thin, flat piece of wood or other material that is used to cover rooftops

tuft (TUHFT)—a bunch of hair

wagging (WAG-ing)—to quickly move something from side to side

wail (WALE)—to let out a long cry of sadness

Discussion Questions

1. Colin felt guilty for being jealous of the attention his brother received from his parents. What could his parents have done to make Terry's arrival into the family less stressful for Colin?

2. Foreshadowing occurs when authors give clues about something that might happen later in a story. How did the author foreshadow that Colin was not an ordinary boy?

3. The explosion destroyed the house, yet Jamie is determined that he and his parents will rebuild. Why do you think he is determined to stay at the site of the explosion?

Writing Prompts

1. Colin became so angry at his brother that he wanted to hurt him. Was there ever a time that a family member made you so angry you felt like you could hurt them? Write about what happened.

2. Even though he's a ghost, Colin dreams of flying and being free. Write about a problem that you want, or once wanted, to be free of.

3. Colin could not stop feeling guilty. Describe a time that you felt guilty about something you said or did. How did you get rid of your guilt?

Internet Sites

Do you want to know more about subjects related to this book? Or are you interested in learning about other topics? Then check out FactHound, a fun, easy way to find Internet sites.

Our investigative staff has already sniffed out great sites for you!

Here's how to use FactHound:

1. Visit *www.facthound.com*

2. Select your grade level.

3. To learn more about subjects related to this book, type in the book's ISBN number: **1598891030**.

4. Click the **Fetch It** button.

FactHound will fetch the best Internet sites for you!